RED VELVET

RED VELVET

POEMS

SHORT STORIES

BY

THOMAS DECKER

CONTENTS

RED VELVET

RED VELVET

Red Velvet was her name

Her colors drawn in the NYC Subway

There's a gas station near where the boys stole the liquor

Velvet looks out her apartment window

She wishes she didn't have to go

Bright lights and a hand down under

Hallucinations and passing out after

Velvet throws away her cigarette

Her colors on the house's floor

Tears painted on the door

Sneaking in the night

A door open

A road with a flaming trail

America's hypocrites!

Parties for the masochists!

Pitch black in the parking lot!

Words sprung!

Love no one!

Arizona's sunsets splatter the skyline with creamy yellow

LA's skyscrapers are greeters to the cheery clouds

Freedom is the priceless air that is breathed through arms and legs

He saw her standing there

Lonely at the Cafe on East 13th St

Black Pearl was his name

Black seated next to Red

He wonders what pleasure has brought all this pain

What circumstance left a trail of paint?

Two beautiful shades are splattered on the walls of grey

Black Pearl caresses this lovely medication

He's a pearl with a crack

His rage had marched through a colorless parade

Finally, color is here to splatter with the dark

Red Velvet runs her rosy lips down a shadowy neck

Black Pearl locks a crimson corsage inside his oily dark heart

The darkness holds on like quicksand till the light complies with a laugh

Red Velvet clinging to a soul stuck in midnight

As if she were a koala clinging to a tree

Black and Red splatter again and again

Till the bed is a painting so freshly wet

Laughs all night begging for more

Night after night till the joy is sore

Early morning

White light rips gently through the curtains

Past portraits will always mix with their new colors

Black Pearl stays entranced by euphoric dreams of seductive scarlet

Red Velvet closes the curtains

Like a cell mate who hates reminders of what she could've seen

The colors she chose to absorb instead

Sunlight wants to serve

A lock is chocked, beat, and pulled

The darkness awoken

A ghoulishly arousing hand snaps hard

A desire shouting

Black's fear returning

Roots cry black

He wasn't always this way

Red knows she needs to feel a breeze

Black is afraid he'll lose the temporary cure

A hand on a chest is felt

Persuasion is a dangerous painting

Black and Red is splattered once more

Is this all Red Velvet is meant for?

An erotic joy to burn her shades bright?

No

Sneaking in the night

Door opened

A road with a flaming trail

Ms. Crimson is coming down the alleyway

Ms. Crimson is her name and she'll burn it on your wall

A maddening revenge that zip lines right into a broken heart

Ms. Crimson will make sure you know her revolution

An evolution of violence and banners hung in the lonely winter

Ms. Crimson is on the run

A revolution struck down

The darkest black can't be fought with the darkest crimson

The shades just mix and paint all night

An orange hue

A portrait burnt in a remorseful flame

CRIMSON REVOLUTION

Red Velvet is sentenced to the orange flames of confinement

She paints many portraits on her concrete walls

Filled with numbers, days, and data of the madhouse

The scurrying of the rats

Their teeth clattering away

Forms a stonier melody than what you would hear on the outside

Cause the lights barely flicker from evening to midnight

Leaving the rats to their own devices

While Velvet's colors seep away

Into the numbers on the wall

There was a morning of shouts and screams

Crimson blood left self-proclaimed scriptures of revolution

Bars were broken

Concrete flying through the air like the decapitation of the tallest mountain

A deed done by TNT

Erupted by a most unstable gunpowder

An angered desire for the bloodiest justice

Red Velvet dances through the chaos

Rock n Roll is all she hears in her mental atmosphere

The revolution has begun

A Crimson Revolution

BLACK PEARL

Black Pearl continued the search

For a medicine so pure

With lips like the sunset

And legs of a cheetah

The lovely opioid of her submission

Abandoned Pearl with his withdrawals

Sweat, laughs, and tears of oil

Black Pearl questions his canvas of tattoos

Mirrors

Truths

Hallways

Black

Is all he sees

Black Pearl, you sing to the shadows of the trees

Black Pearl, you lie to the stars in the lake

Everyone is a rolling stone

The stone takes shape and starts rolling away

DOME

A revolution fueled a battle cry

The setting sun glowed a golden flare upon the city's newly spilled red tint

Red Velvet is the name carved on the streets

Currency gutted from the bellies of the nobles

Tongues of the wise beaten into submission to the leash

Like a dog being stripped from its kennel

And learning to live in a dome

Not a home

Revolutions are born with the lust for victory

And permanent reform to appease the crackling castles amongst us all

Most pity those with the euphoric sense of success

Cause we're all aware of the void that arrives soon

Knocking on the dome

Glowing under the cabins

Greeting the Red during the day to day love

THE VOID RISING

Black Pearl awaits the gathering of colors

From where red shades were rejected

Or splashed onto portraits

Black Pearl recollected the nights of gushing hues

Velvet crying for more

Thrust after thrust she laughed and gushed freshly wet red

With a taint of black that never faded away

The colleagues of colors snap their leader out of the past

Black is aware of his imprint on The Crimson's pain

A revolution, as we know, sprouts from the seeds of rage

But can an uprising sprouting from the weeds of regret

Defeat a regime powered by a forest of rage?

COLORS IN WAR

Red, Black, Green, Blue, Yellow, Grey, Indigo, Pink, Orange, Purple, White

Colors in war

Colors in death

No colors at rest

Portraits painted in bloodshed

Two leaders

Two worlds

No deeds in the past can be atoned to

Bloody portraits imprinted on the rocks of the Earth

Have tiled the battlefield like a home under construction

The forever home for the hounds

Barking their loud remorse into their forever soil

CRIMSON OR RED?

Blood spilt to write the anthems

Sung by choirs dressed in orange and spears

Glass is shattered with no purpose woven through logic

But rather a spontaneous deed

Cause fear sprouts from the unknown like a puppy lost in the wilderness

its owner nowhere near to supply the living creature with the warmth of

certainty

The warmth of a path

The warmth of a plan

Velvet's voice lacks from the songs

Bloodshed, while satisfying, is a revolution lacking a conclusion

Lacking the climax

Slow to the reality

DOVES

"Have you seen Red Velvet's crown?

She smashed its gold and cracked her throne."

"Does she not desire the newly grown throne? Painted by beggars brought

down from the sky-scraping towns?"

"Not one Crimson soldier will reveal more of her lore. We best shut our

mouths before the Crimsons cut the doves!"

PORTRAIT OF ASHES

The nation grows a crimson glow

Elder graves lack stones to mark the portrait's ashes of pearl white

Youthful soldiers are born within walls

Shot down Blackbirds are what the children hear

Metallic defenses are the children's lives

Red Velvet gazes upon her regime

The Elite burning under the gauntlet of crimson red judgement

The rule of a crimson red army

The tears of a crimson red queen

Is this what she wanted?

Is this justice ripe like a fruitful harvest?

And right like a lover's comforting warmth letting Velvet know she can't be

hurt any longer?

A lover

A lover!

Is this power not a newly wedded lover?

Is this empire not a dome to lock out the fears as the portraits locked out her

No

Velvet refused to believe these ideas

They clawed at her brain like a rabid dog to a rabbit

A scream slashed its way up Velvet's throat

A fate of weakness meant for a woman dressed in dread

Painted in questions

Molested by fear

The flames tongued the throne

The fire fondled the banners

The destruction had no limits in this castle of a personal hell

Although

Red Velvet's portrait has begun anew

Not a portrait with life

But a portrait of ashes

REMEMBER

In a town baring scars as clear as a lake

Cars whiz by like there's a treasure to take

A boy reads a story

Quite gruesome

Quite dark

And illustrated in red

The boy is not tall

Just merely a seed in this city

Eager to grow

But easy to crush

The boy leaves the bookstore to hurry home for food

But comes across a man

His shadow as black as his eyes

His skin flowed like smoke in the air

But remained a stormy thick like deadly Neptune clouds

The man warned the boy not to mutter the name around his tired, hazy eyes

The pain of its power can lead the man to realize

That his lies to the air have been pacts muttered in vain

The pain inflicted on this land had been ignited by his hand

Through the pain of what the man perceived as love

Is what inspired her hate

Her fabricated sense of justice

Her Crimson Justice

The boy, confused, walks on with his book

The man, torn up, walks down into the bright city day

Full of sunshine, smiles, no regime to be seen

Maybe, one day, the man can shine again

Like a pearl on the seashore

Black

Like the night

Poetry/ short story collection continues next page

WHIP CREAM

Trees are a server

Of notions and slime

Concrete's a lover

Of fine dines and wine

Sad is a comfort food

All on its own

The sky is a moderator

Given the cold

Taste the whip cream left on my head

I'll eat yours

But not till we're dead

The ocean's a country

Calling for war

The water's cigar lets you question your sores

Sad's a comfort food

I'll say it again

And over and over

Till us both are dead

LAKE

The world may not know of the darkness in my walls

Inked by whispers, trembling, and echoes of their messages

Sewers stream through historical plight

ortraits ring a bell to signal the rain of erotic shame down onto the wandering

neighbors of the plains

Fingers point from the popcorn walls

Machetes swing from the ends of pens

Save me!

Save me!

The night is still young!

29

But we all realize how crystal clear the lake has become

TOMMY'S POEM

You know I often wonder where my voice truly belongs

Like a puppy in the rain suffering from the pain of having no bark to display

My drums speak for themselves through a medium of bashing, cracking,

snapping and more

But was that voice enough to keep her attention span?

My plan on a blueprint printed

spat unconditionally onto her lips of tragedy!

Tell me why your wings soar

I'm a pigeon with a mission without permission of love itself!

Just tell me why saying "I love you" spawns the horrors of my heart and lies

inside your fault lines

Loving you was a warm fireplace

Then we all burst into a wildfire

<u>LAUGH</u>

"HAHAHAHAHAHAHAHAHA!"

That laugh is still with me. It needs to go away. It needs to go away. It wasn't

my fault. I wanted to save her. I FUCKIN TRIED!"

"Honey!"

Sammy is snapped back to reality; his hair drenched in cold, dripping sweat.

His face a bloody pulp from all the tearing

"Babe, it wasn't your fault."

"YES, IT FUCKING WAS, BITCH!" Sammy roared at his terrified wife wit

every ounce of anger and frustration festering up in his mind. Sammy knew h

should've done more for her; instead, he engorged himself into the shadows

hoping to strike a match. How foolish Sam felt.

How cowardly Sam was.

"We couldn't stop her addiction... not even the Big Man could do anything"

Rose reasoned.

"Oh yeah, fuckin working with LOCAL GANGS IS GOING TO SHOUT,

'DON'T DO DRUGS KIDDIES!' DO YOU EVEN HEAR YOURSELF! WI

TOLD THEM TO KEEP HER AWAY FROM DRUGS AT ALL COSTS!

WE EVEN TOLD THEM TO KEEP HER HOSTAGE! WHAT THE FUCK

WAS THAT SUPPOSED TO PROTECT HER?"

"WE COULDN'T AFFORD FUCKIN REHAB MOTHERFUCKER!"

Rose was starting to lose her sanity as well. She wanted the noise to stop; she needed the noise to stop. Yes, The Big Man brutally gutted her daughter's innards out like she was a pig awaiting slaughter. It was how he punished Sammy for not having the money to pay him for his services. Sammy came home furious, beating Rose, almost killing her. She was the one responsible for the lack of funds because of all those nights at the casino. Rose had been getting in deep with the sharks. She couldn't stop, the excitement of the game was addictively thrilling. She never dreamed of having her bothersome daughter get in the way of her fun, until there was no longer a daughter to be bothered by.

"WHATEVER! I need to go to the restroom"

Sammy left his wife alone in the darkness of their motel room. Left her alone to contemplate her grief. Left her alone to realize her selfishness. Left her alone to realize her greed. Left her alone to realize her failure.

Rose still remembered her daughter's smile; warm but shuddering, full but hollow. She was Sammy's whole world, Rose's too; or was she?

This question had been whispering in Rose's ears her whole parenthood. Every time she sees a dollar, she hears it. Every time she lays in bed, she hears it. The question often makes Rose giggle in her pillow. Sammy would always ask her to shut up every night, but Rose would always respond the same "You have to laugh every once in a while, to stay sane in this circus act of a life".

Sammy would respond with a punch to her gut and the lighting of a cigarette.

When their daughter brought meth to the front door, the house was never silent from that point on. Screams echoed through every millisecond of the day. Insanity is never too far behind those noises, not too far behind at all. Especially when all she hears is the laugh, all night, every beautiful night.

"Hehehehehehehe."

"Babe, what's so fuckin funny?"

"Hehehehehe."

"Babe?"

Sammy was at a loss for words. The look on Rose's face was inhuman.

She had eyes weeping profusely.

She had a smile laughing grotesquely

It was as if Rose couldn't decide whether to grieve or to forget. Whether this

was all real or just a bad gag, a cold punchline. Whether to scream curses int

the air at her daughter's killer or laugh like this is all a sick. Twisted. Bad.

Joke.

Rose, however, found bad jokes amusing occasionally; even funny!

She recollected how silly her daughter's liver looked hanging out of her gut.

How she looked so dorky with nail heads for eyes. How comical she looked

without any hands.

It was all so funny

So

Incredibly

Funny

"HAHAHAHAHAHAHAHAHAHAHAAAAAAAA!"

"SHUT THE FUCK UP!" Sammy cried.

There was something about this form of insanity.

It was almost hypnotic.

"HAHAHAHAHAHAHAHAHAHA!"

Sammy attempted to cover his ears, but it finally hit him, it all made sense.

Sammy wanted to cry, but instead, he laughed.

"Hehehehehe... HAHAHAHAHAHAHA!"

Sammy wailed in gut wrenching laughter.

"HAHAHAHAHAHAHAHAHA!"

Rose wailed back.

The couple finally felt better. They finally saw the funny side of it all. Ha ha

ha ha ha ha ha.

<u>TWITCH</u>

This urge is almost inhuman

Twitchy days are what define my movement

Oh look, a new collection of bruises

Just another day

Just another complaint

Please don't notice

You saw nothing

Quick, I need to ignore the assumptions

Just act natural

I hear the staring

Just keep walking

It's just another day

41

My bones

are yelping

My throat

Is searing

My brain

Is begging

Begging me to get more sleep

But at night I can explore with no eyes on me

But there comes the urge

Bruises and pain

Resilience throwing in the towel again

I'm sorry

I'll hold it in

Hold in the anthill crawling on my organs and skin

My ants crawl out

And back in again

I'm shivering

Shaking

You don't need demons to be possessed

But don't worry, I'll try

It's just another day

Oh look, a new collection of bruises

THE SILENCE

Graduated

Yay

Oh, what a happy day

All these pythons in one room

Lying through their fangs like Hilary Clinton in the pages

Oh, I know you

You knew me too

The silence at night tugs on the chords of your brain

The amplifiers can't sing for days

A girl that my poems refuse to let go of

I've faced the silence too

I've been on that planet as well

I've viewed the mascara dripping down your leg

I've witnessed you crying to the mirror that's trapped in slumber

When you kissed him

Did you think of me?

When he caressed your breast

Did you think of me?

When you tasted his fangs

Did you think of me?

When you held me

Did the Silence whisper through my touch?

<u>ALONE</u>

Being alone is scary enough

But Alone with My Thoughts is a terrifying title for a horror movie

Staying up till 2 am did nothing for my fears

But exhaustion will always serve as my pain killer

Cause tick tock goes the clock of when my reality should be a dreamland

But I guess The Sandman decided my slumber was not a priority

Maybe Jack Frost visited instead to freeze over my undead memories

I never realized that killing my mind for the night was the world's new

extreme sport until now

I see that it's only 12 o clock

Not enough brain cells have died to numb me up

So, I continue through the night like a ferris wheel

Up and down

Left to right

Back and forth

Over and over again

OVER AND OVER AGAIN

Candles are lit

Hot as white

While we were here

She taught me to cry

I'll hate myself

Better than you

My sweat is ensnared

So, what can I do?

You live in the sky

No one can lie

The blackest roses sit with the graves

A howl creeps into laughter

Salamanders crawl into the ears

Dragging along the ants and tarantulas

Ownership of the body is a game now

A vessel

A throne

UNIVERSE OF LOVE

I knew I couldn't hide my love for long

I knew the tidal waves would knock the word right out

A dress of soothing black

Hands softer than the evening wind

Words that soar right off her page

Stories that know her past as a sage

An angelic crown welcomed light to the dance floor

But not even the sun can outmatch the galaxies in her smile

The planets in her stories

The love in my poems

Alas, I know my love will remain a mere dream

A book containing no tales

Love was never rational

Love was never fair

My pen only desires her grace

A longing for which no man can paralyze

I'm aware my pen has no home on your universe

But allow me to gift you with a sentence

A sentence revealing the writing on the wall

That you're the one and only love of my life

But I'll respect your wishes

And keep my love stowed away

But my galaxies will always be here

For you

Forever

MOVE ON

The beauty drove me mad

You're finally here and I can't speak

Barely look you in the eye

Enjoy my hand in yours

My arms around your torso

One sided love is enough to trigger lunacy

No, I can't move on from her creamy cocoa hair

I can't move on from her penmanship, worthy to be recited by the heavens

can't move on from her daydreamy curls, her Saint Teresa like compassion

I'll never move on from her

Not cause I don't want to

53

But because I'll never be able to

<u>FUTURE</u>

The backstage reeks of restlessness

Suspense kickstarts my heart

The crowd chaotically demands a behemoth of sound

My drumsticks ache from the rigidity of my warmup

Sweat storms down my neck

Gargantuan tsunamis of chants impact the dressing room

The moment preys near

The music grinds its talons to perfection

The stage thunders an awakening of aureate light

Our trail to the stage begins

Our brotherhood detonates to life

Our band

Our future

Our life

The drum set awaits my embrace like a patient lover

The crowd's eyes widen with unbreakable awe

The cue is given

The song demands an imperishable hypnosis

The stadium loses self-control

And the beauteous chaos begins

HOMECOMING

Dark haired women with the crown of an angel

She's a beautiful queen from the land of the stage

Your lips speak of dreams and futures

I'm not part of your planned mixture

But now you know where my heart falls in the pot

Take this confession how you will

Spill my blood or let it flow

Down the drain or down your heart

Dark haired girl with a smile smoother than the clouds

She's a magical woman that knows not to whom my heart bleeds

All those classes in high school I fell asleep in

But now I can hardly close my eyes

STARS

I can hold your hand while we sit below a starry night

I can write our story on the wall

Flowers in your hair will fit quite nicely, don't you agree?

When we walk alone at midnight

Below the starry black sky

I'll teach you the constellations

The direction of Venus and Mars

I'll whisper into your lips

How our love will travel the cosmos

With a kiss on your rosy red lips

And a pluck of my jet-black guitar

We'll float into the night

Like a dream of endless light

PIZZA

I felt like writing a song with pizza mentioned in it

Maybe I'll write something clever about girls soaked in soft neon light

Why do rhymes pull me backwards when they're glorified poetically

I guess I don't know where to place my verse

I'll rehearse

She doesn't know I'm a poet

Oh, here I'm going again

Writing about the latest girl

Offering words without offering her name

Maybe pizza is the inspiring word of the day

Telling me to eat the crust before my songs bite the dust

I guess hunger has a hold on my desire

On my words for her to admire

But after all

Pizza is the only inspiring word of the day

IF

If a girl is beautiful

You tell her

If a girl is wonderful

You show her

If a girl is colorful

Paint her

If a girl is all three

Write about her

Write about her dreams

Write about her goals

Write about her stories

Write about her worlds

And when the writing has been done

And the sun has escaped into slumber

Show her the writing

If the words tickle her smile

And the metaphors ignite the stars in her eyes

Then you'll know

She's happy

I WANNA END ME

I wanna end me

End all fights on my trail

It's like I'm looking for dungeons

With bricks made of candles and floor made with glass

Am I born to be a beast?

Neutral to happiness and pain

Having no preference

Numb to my smile

Dipped in a scorching blood

Cries from all the cities above

I wanna end me

<u>SEA</u>

Can we build a house out of oxygen?

I'll supply my breath to build our castle

All I ask for is scuba gear

Cause your mysteries are like water

Filling my lungs with hopes and dreams

That'll pull me down like an anchor in the sea

I don't need saving

The elements decide my fate

Cause fear is like water

Until we utter the final statement

And black is all we know in the sea so deep

THE DEATH SENATE

Death doesn't please the ground

Relief leader's worries

Open cell doors

Or save the damsel crying on the street corner

Death contorts

Death steals

Death gropes

Death contracts

Death sings no cheers to human rights

Death decays love and empathy

Death is our truly frightening law

67

CANDLELIGHT

The writer strangles his tongue till blood is dug up

An organ drenched in red

A social declaration

Praising silence

Submitting to beauteous withdrawal

It's so tempting to water down the thoughts with words smuggled by silence

The tongue seems useless in the pursuit of creativity

But the writer will soon regret the strategic strangulation

When Voice cracks the mystery

And conversations revere new paths through candlelight

WAITING

Waiting for the moment to confess

The time that'll be ripe to ignite my love for her fright

Like a moth to a light

So, I snap my ribs

Reach deep through my lungs

And missiles of wet red splurge onto our dying soil

Desperate for such a beauteous elixir of human production

The fresh red

The freshly dead

Finally

The heart has been reached

Is this the love she desires?

My heart can't leave as well

she knows life's desires

The fruits mocking our tongues

Why can't my blood please your lungs!

I never needed yours

EMERALD

An emerald night

Above her heavy metal heart

Pearl eyes

Above a silky soft smile

Holding her hand is a privilege

One I hope she'll grant to me

Out of a pure, shining love

Like a candle lit by infernos

Ensnared by the strings of her rightful control

"My dear, may I hold you close for this one dance?

Do I deserve such an honor? Your fingers stroking through mine?

Like two pythons joining in a tail entangled danger?

Cause love is risky

Like a lighter in a cabin

But don't you fear

Flames die down

Emeralds shape dreams

<u>RIDDLE</u>

On date night a girl never has to remember her pocketknife, but Mom thought otherwise. Cheryl didn't think her relationship was a safety risk emotionally or physically; Todd was such a sweet guy, handsome too.

He was always so loving, caring, and smelled like spring flowers at the foot of an aqua blue pond. Cheryl's father once met Todd at a 4th of July barbecue a mutual friend was hosting. After a few failed attempts of humor from Todd and tons of backhanded compliments from Dad; Cheryl's father ever stopped referring to her beloved as the "black cat that crossed her path". black cats had sleek leather jackets, bowl cuts, and a shy smile then that's a at species Cheryl wasn't aware of. The tragedy of this all, however, was how high school movies encouraged romanticized promises of nice boys in tuxes and slow ballroom dances. They never mentioned overprotective mom style

security checks.

"Do you have your phone?"

"Yes, mom"

Cheryl, to not roll her eyes, used every bittersweet drop of willpower stored in her soul. Unfortunately, Cheryl couldn't repress a slight, sassy, frustrated ruffle of her bright blonde hair. Cheryl began to walk closer to the door, hoping she could rush past the questionnaire. Mother, noticed this, and greatly amped the intensity of the pre-date night interrogations. It was almost scary how ferociously the questions shot like cannonballs, leaving red stains

on Cheryl's mental stamina.

"Do you have your phone? Wallet? Pepper spray? Pocket knife?".

"MOTHER!"

Mom's eyes transitioned from drivingly caring to distraught and tearful. She wanted so bad to caution her daughter, to let her know she can't hide all secrets forever. Cheryl knew what she did was wrong, and Mom knew she didn't need reminding. The fear, however, was the reality whispering in Mom's ear with a deep, slithery amusement. Todd would find out. He'll know.

The truth cuts a man's heart deeper.

Much deeper.

"Oh, mom... I didn't-".

"No, it's quite alright... I... um. This boy's nice to you... um... Just keep your guard up. Once he finds out about-".

"He won't find out! Todd trusts me! He would never suspect anything!

"But do you feel shame? Do you feel no guilt?".

"Of course, I do!"

Cheryl was quick to fire back at her mother's concerns. A flame of

burning passion growing from the roots of a young girl's fear. Cheryl didn't

mean for such a storm of abrasiveness to be rained down upon her mother; but

the instinct grew stronger, the instinct to protect. The need to guard the

worries, weaknesses, and secrets. That's what fear does to its hosts; it either

distorts reality or sharpens it like a knife.

"Mom... it'll be alright. I know Todd is a little weird, but he would ever hurt me." Cheryl reasoned, feeling the guilt continue to trickle down her rosy lips, leading to her excitable tongue, and falling down her dirty throat.

"Just watch, Todd and I will have tons of fun tonight and everything will be alright, ok?"

Mother didn't feel any more comfortable with that reassurance. Her old eyes took their gaze away from her daughter and down to the ground. Mother continued to sit silently in a mental pit of extreme skepticism, running through the terrible possibilities of tonight's upcoming events. Her daughter sat perfectly still, urgently awaiting a response from a silent parent. Sweat trickled down Cheryl's short, blue dress. A deadly silence

A deadly void.

Todd was the boy Cheryl occasionally hid in the backyard. Todd was the boy who gifted Cheryl with her first kiss. Todd was the boy who brought Cheryl on her first ever date. All those events were uniformed in the dreamy replication of a fairytale; however, all stories have their pitfalls. Most storylines would reveal the female's chosen prince as a plotting mastermind of all things mischievous; revealing a worthier prince by the end of the story. Cheryl's story, however, is different; much different. Wickedness can twist a story like a tongue stuttering on its alibis.

"Just keep your secret. You may think you know Todd but you never truly know a man until-"

"You talk like you know Todd, but you don't!" Cheryl screamed, interrupting her mother. "You really don't. Don't you ever talk like you do!".

"I don't know Todd, but I know your father".

What? Dad is... well... Dad. What are you talking about?" Cheryl asked, with sweat continuing to drip down her face.

"Look, just go on your date. You'll have a fun time. Keep me updated, ok?" Mom ordered.

Cheryl didn't know how to respond to such vague connections, especially about her own father! Mom and Dad have been together for 29 years! Cheryl never witnesses harsh fights between them, ever! Yes, Dad loathed Mom's homemade pizza; Mom despised Dad spending money on toy car collectibles, but those were minor things. A strong couple would never have a meltdown over those tiny tussles. To be fair, what Cheryl had done was more than a ussle, it was a monstrosity. The only comforting thought during the walk to

Todd's house was that he didn't need to know. Not absolutely everything ha

to be shared in a committed relationship, right?

After 15 minutes of walking in the cool fall breeze, Cheryl had reached

Todd's house; a larger sized, upper-middle-class home. The interior reeked c

wet paint but had a beauteous pearly white glow that nobody could miss. Tod

has always been confident of his talents and refused having his humble abod

touched by hired workers. Todd's parents were perplexed by this sudden cry

for independence but were aware of Todd's talent. Cheryl would often gush

over him skillfully wielding his majestic paintbrush; like a virgin desiring tc

tear her man's covers to enter conjoined oblivion of lovemaking. The color

Todd chose was green, however, the Homeowner's Association didn't find

this the least bit appealing. Todd was cursing the association for weeks after

the painting had to be redone to white.

Cheryl admired her boyfriend's handiwork before ringing the doorbe

but after one ring the door stays closed. Cheryl rings it one more time but wi no result. The pearly white door just sits closed with the eerily quiet breeze passing by. The image of Todd bursting through the door with a paintbrush in his hand was all that Cheryl wanted right now; it was what she needed.

"Maybe he's asleep, he did work hard on this house. But isn't this where he wanted to see me? What if he found out? No no no... definitely not."

Cheryl's mind continued to go in a million directions and to every worst possible assumption. She began to review everything that has happened while planning this date; maybe to serve as a distraction or to realize something she had forgotten.

Todd had told her a couple of days ago to meet him at his house. They were planning on driving to a five-star restaurant to celebrate Todd's finished work on the house. Both were heading to college in the fall; Cheryl to technical school and Todd to art school. Tonight, would be one of the last dates they would enjoy together for a couple of months. For that reason, Todd promised

tonight would be special. Cheryl promised she'd remember tonight forever.

But the door wasn't opening

The doorbell wasn't ringing

Cheryl started sweating

Her hand pushed the door.

"Hey... babe."

Cheryl's eyes darted to the living room window a few feet from the front

door. She couldn't see Todd's face, or even identify that there was a figure

near the glass.

"Um... hey handsome! I can't see where you're at... are you painting? You really gotta leave your paintings more often; I can't see your sexy face when you're busy-"

"Cheryl...It's not a painting, babe. It's actually... um... a surprise. I won't see you for a long freaking time, so I wanted to make something sweet for you to remember me by in college... I don't expect anything in return... only your happiness. I love you so freakin much, Cheryl."

Todd's voice was a timid, thin string of words. He seemed nervous, almost afraid. But the smoothness of Todd's dialect sprung up enduring images and memories sweet like candy canes. The leather jackets in the freezing winter, starry skies on the sleepless nights, and purely naked love in the summer evenings.

"And where would I find this surprise?"

Cheryl asked this question in her own thin, timid voice. A hungry attempt to replicate the seductive words of another, to achieve an award only the seduced desire.

"In the backyard... you're going to love it. It's something you'll never forget" Todd replied.

"Alrighty, babe."

Cheryl took her first steps towards the backyard's gate. Each step springing jolts of girly giddiness up her spine. What romantic gifts were waiting in there? Flowers? Chocolate? Flowers AND Chocolate? Cheryl attempted to savor this moment by stepping ever so slowly, but excitement took the whee

Cheryl sprinted to Todd's backyard like a dog to a treat. Her mouth giggling, her skirt flailing, her love swelling. But much to Cheryl's annoyance, an extremely dense wall of bushes awaited Cheryl a few feet past the gate. She looked to the right and left but couldn't find a way past the monstrous vegetation.

"Cheryl! The entrance is all the way to the right! I'll meet you there, beautiful!"

Cheryl could hear Todd's voice coming from past the bushes. She desperately desired to ask question after question but excitement grabbed ahold of her. Cheryl sprinted to the right of the bushes, and after a couple minutes of hard jogging, the entrance came into sight. A circular hole in the bushes with white flowers surrounding the outline. To describe this entrance as welcoming, considering its beauty, would be an understatement. Cheryl began to consider that maybe all her excitement really was worth it. She trusted this gift

awaiting her came from Todd's heart, his loving heart.

Cheryl went through the opening with a bright grin and fell to the floor in

shocking dismay. The view in front of her was breathtakingly sadistic and

horrifyingly stunning. Cheryl had to hold back the urge to vomit, she wasn't

successful.

In the middle of the yard was the head of Todd's yellow Labrador Retriever

The head's snout was facing toward the cloudy sky of fall. The tongue was

sticking out the side of the mouth with a sharp stick keeping it firm to the

ground. The grass surrounding the head was painted a chalky shade of white

Cheryl wanted to scream.

She needed to scream.

"AAAAAAAAAAAHHHHHHHHH!"

The tears sprang from Cheryl's eyes like bombs over a monument. She desperately curled up into a ball, hoping this was all just a nightmare. Cheryl closed her eyes, imagining her beloved mother waking up the treasured daughter of the house. Mother's aged dimples glistening in the morning sun's golden aura, while Cheryl's honey blonde hair rises out of the shadow of lumber. A cozy, warm hug is shared between the two; mother then whispers in Cheryl's ear with words softer than silk.

"There's no need to cry, no need to fear, mother's here to hold you near and dear. I won't hurt you and Todd will save you.

Cause Todd's a nice boy.

Todd is a great man.

YOU BITCH!"

"WAKE UP, BITCH!"

Cheryl is sucker punched right in the mouth. Blood spurts from her lip but she doesn't cry, she knows Todd will save her; her emotions are too drained to think otherwise. Cheryl looks around to find herself chained to a wall with her arms above her in an awkward position. Her legs were chained to an object in the shadows that Cheryl could not identify. The grotesqueness of her surroundings only worsened when the smell of rotten flesh infected the air inside what seemed to be a dark, vacant basement. The walls were colored a deathly gray from what Cheryl could tell. The room was so wide and dark that it was impossible to accurately survey her surroundings.

"Where had that punch come from? Where is my fuckin kidnapper? In this room? Right near me? WHERE IS HE?"

These thoughts raced through Cheryl's mind like cars in an arcade game.

"Fuck! Fuck! Fuck! Ok think positively! Todd will rescue me any moment

now. He will jump through the window like Batman saving a damsel in

distress. It'll happen any fuckin second now!"

These positive thoughts held back the tears for a few minutes, but ultimately

harshly failed. But not one tear could secrete from her eyes before Cheryl's

name was screamed once more.

"Look at me Cheryl, LOOK AT ME!"

Cheryl's head jolted up to see a man sitting punching distance away from her.

His face was smeared with white paint, his eyes were littered with dried tears,

and his clothes were a torn-up Anthrax t-shirt along with basketball shorts.

The two sat in silence for what seemed an eternity, but, the silence added up

to just a few minutes of cold, dead staring. Cheryl recognized that shirt, she desperately wished she hadn't. The man sniffed Cheryl's blood on his wrist; swollen grin followed shortly after. The look in his eyes displayed an erotic pleasure from tasting the rapid fear that was coursing through his victim's blood like lightning through a rod. The man then walked into the darkness far and sporadically like a moth to a light. Cheryl couldn't decide what to feel; massive relief for alone time to escape, or a grim dread of facing reality. These thoughts of indecisiveness were interrupted by ear shattering screams originating from the shadows Cheryl's leg chains led into.

"AAAAAAHHHHHHHHHH"

"T-t-t-"

"TODD! TODD! I'M FUCKING TODD!"

"B-baby what happened to you? Why am I chained? WHY DID YOU

PUNCH ME?"

Cheryl is sucker punched once more, but this time in the eye.

"Allow me to show you WHY!"

Todd ran quickly into the shadows where a blood curdling scream from an

unknown man followed shortly after. His screaming continued and slowly

manifested into sobbing. The chains attached to Cheryl's legs started to move

towards her, causing her to scream internally. A bloody man wearing a white

t- shirt and jeans then came running out of the darkness towards Cheryl. He

had short, brown hair and a certain glow to his eyes that Cheryl, much to her

horror, recognized. The man had deep stab wounds on his arms, cuts on his face, but fortunately not much damage to his legs. Cheryl then looked down to realize her leg chains were attached to Danny's legs as well.

"DANNY!"

"CHERYL!"

Todd, using much of the energy he had left, grabs Danny by his collar. He then holds out a knife that was undoubtably used to torture Danny. Todd's arm raised the weapon above his head, getting ready to strike.

"STOP!"

Todd pauses his motion and pounces onto Cheryl's terror by giving her a

deadly stare. Cheryl knew those eyes, they used to be different, much

different.

"You don't want him! You want me! I'M THE ONE WHO CHEATED ON

YOU FOR ALL OF HIGH SCHOOL! I'M THE ONE WHO LIED TO YOU

OVER AND OVER AGAIN! DON'T KILL HIM! KILL ME!" Cheryl's tears

poured onto her dress like the Niagara Falls on a summer's day. She hoped

Todd was believing this testimony.

Todd walked over to Cheryl while still holding on to Danny. Cheryl's

scandalous lover wanted so desperately to fight back but was bleeding

profusely from his wounds. Whatever Cheryl was going to do she needed to

do it fast.

"I could kill you... but that wouldn't be nearly as satisfying. I have plans for both of you... big plans... fun plans. A-a-a-and I'll make examples of you! And no one will ever lie to me ever again! EVER! EVER! NEVER AGA-AAHHHHHHHHHHHH!"

Todd had been stabbed behind the knee by Danny using Cheryl's pocketknife. Apparently, during the time Danny was in her sight she took the sudden risk of dropping her weapon. Todd was now moaning on the cold, rough concrete floor. Danny then stabbed both off Todd's hands so he couldn't fight back. Blood gushed from the maniac's hands like a popped water balloon. A huge gunk of Todd's thick, red, inner liquids sprayed onto Danny's face. The urge to vomit sprinted its way up and expelled itself onto Todd's furious expression.

"YOU BITCH! YOU BITCH!" Todd wailed.

"GET ME OUTTA HERE!" Cheryl screamed.

Danny, being a man of few words, simply did as he was told. Danny grabbed whatever keys he could find from Todd's pockets and tried them on Cheryl's chains. The arm chains were successfully unlocked but the leg chains were a different story.

GET UP! WE'LL HAVE TO RUN OUT OF HERE STILL ATTACHED TO EACH OTHER!"

Danny could've waited for Cheryl's answer, but he refused. Danny picked her up and ran up the stairs, past the living room, and out the front door. Tons of furniture had been pushed over by the chains, but Danny couldn't give less of a darn. Todd's voice could still be heard from downstairs, he shouted words that sent chills down Danny's spine.

"YOU CAN'T GET AWAY! I HAVE EYES ALL AROUND! THERE'S

MORE TO THIS INSANITY THAN YOU REALIZE, MOTHERFUCKER

JUST ASK CHERYL'S UPSTANDING GENTLEMAN OF A FATHER! H.

HA HA HA HAAAA HA HA HA!"

Once outside Danny called 911. It didn't take long for the cops and an

ambulance to arrive once the situation was explained to them. Danny,

somehow finding humor in that horrific mess, found amusing how Todd

didn't even think to take his cell phone away.

"What an idiot. If you're going to kill someone at least put some thought into

it, Todd ol' boy" Danny thought to himself.

The ambulance brought both Danny and Cheryl to the hospital to be treated. Danny recovered fast with stitches and pain medication, but Cheryl was having the hardest time mentally. She stayed in the hospital for a whole week and it didn't look like she was leaving anytime soon. Danny decided to visit Cheryl one day just to be nice, but she wouldn't talk to him. Cheryl would've conversed with Danny if this was a normal day, but it wasn't. Cheryl wanted to disappear, she wanted to cry river upon river upon river. She didn't know how she was going to move past this or apologize to Danny for getting him into this mess.

"You don't have to feel bad"

"What?"

Cheryl was surprised how well this boy could tell what she was thinking. Maybe after surviving a sociopathic serial killer they had a more unbreakabl bond than before.

"I may be pointing out the obvious, but that guy had issues. Issues you neve had anything to do with. He's a monster, period. And all you did was fuckin cheat on him, and he goes psycho murder crazy on ya. Nothing you did justifies-"

"We did" Cheryl interrupted.

"Okay, nothing we did justifies anything that crazy s.o.b did. You're an amazing person who made a small mistake. That guy was a murderous psych who's going to be in prison for the rest of his damn life.... you see what I mean?"

Cheryl looked into Danny's eyes for perhaps a minute or maybe more before uttering the first sentence she's formed in weeks.

"I love you".

Danny then hugged her until he could feel her heartbeat relaxing like a kitten being stroked gently down its back.

"Now, you get some rest, okay?".

"Okay" Cheryl replied.

Danny stayed in Cheryl's hospital room while Cheryl took the longest, best nap she's taken in weeks. Danny read a magazine on automobiles to entertain himself until Cheryl's dad caught his attention by taping Danny gently on the

shoulder. Danny looked up and saw a rough, wrinkled, old face with a jolly

smile. Cheryl's dad was wearing a flannel, and a pair of khaki jeans being

held up by a thick belt. Danny jumped back in his chair at the sight of this

man. There's only one kind of old man who would be in this room. Todd's

words repeated in Danny's thoughts like a horror movie on replay.

"Just ask Cheryl's upstanding gentlemen of a father! Ha ha ha ha haaaaaa

ha!"

"Oh, you must be Cheryl's dad."

"Yes, I am" he replied. "You and my daughter are all over the news channel.

That bastard Todd tried to kill both of you from what I understand."

"Yeah, he… he lost his mind."

"Well, that's one thing you and I can agree on" Cheryl's father replied.

"Um… what do you mean?" Danny asked.

The old man's jolly smile morphed into a serious frown. He was suspicious of something, but Danny couldn't tell what.

"Let me tell you something, Danny" the old man muttered. "You and I are very similar."

"How so?" Danny asked.

Cheryl's dad laid a hand on Cheryl's dozing body. His face contorted to a wicked smile. A smile that made Danny even more uncomfortable.

"We both know things we wish we never did" He replied.

To be continued....

<u>STORM</u>

My companion, my friend

Why do you sew your clouds tight?

Your cover of grey too mighty for a transparent connection

Your clouds then flew you to distant lands

Same home on a map

But distance only receives understanding from those whose own loneliness

they're still perceiving

I hope you'll fly back

I'll meet you at your doorstep

I won't have clouds of my own

Such a luxury stays in the skies for some

But I hope you can receive my voice through this literature

Perhaps words are my clouds

Or maybe you're a private storm

Opening the tornado for only a few fellows

Made in the USA
Middletown, DE
18 July 2023

34851601R00068